Praise for this book:

None received

The Final Year for Reasonable Hope

Sundodger Books
San Francisco, California

Printed in the United States of America
First edition
ISBN: 979-8-218-24212-1

Contents

Introduction

I hope you enjoy these stories (an objective of mine from the outset). They are set in 2008 and were written then, with multiple exceptions incorporated through the art and science of fraud.

And before I begin, I will concede that a number of positive things have happened since 2008, like improved regard for nurses and the proliferation of food trucks. And some things have held constant since 2008, like the properties of ice and water. But other things got worse – perhaps because we were asking for too much. After all, despite an economic catastrophe, 2008 was a year for optimism. Some may recall the *New York Times* front page headline on November 5, 2008:

OBAMA ELECTED PRESIDENT

RACISM IS OVER

But how could we have foreseen the shitshow to follow? At the time, Donald Trump was a ridiculous public figure, not yet reaching the status of being Vladimir Putin's five-ruble whore.

Reluctantly, however, I will admit that as the world went to hell, my life got better. My amazing wife and I assumed that we were invited to our wedding – and we were right. Without having to appear on Maury Povich, I discovered that I was the father of two wonderful children. And also of note, I found employment that occasionally gives me meaning, not to mention paychecks that lag inflation, but not severely.

Finally, I will mention one last thing: this introduction was written where the stories were written – a rooftop deck above a brewery in Berkeley, California. And at one point in my life, I had hoped to write professionally. But Glenbrook Property Management, Pacific Gas and Electric, the East Bay Municipal Utilities District, the Franchise Tax Board and the Internal Revenue Service thought otherwise. And so, to the aspiring writer by profession, I offer this advice: get a day job, keep it, and never rise to the level of your incompetence. By applying this wisdom personally, I have remained happy with 75 percent of my life.

1. Green Drinks

Last week, I went to San Francisco Green Drinks (a local happy hour for professionals in environmental work) with a few friends and co-workers, halfway hopeful about finding a girlfriend. It took about 30 minutes before resignation set in, although by then I was happy to spend time with everyone whom I knew. But of course, as always, a young professional on a networking spree had to interrupt a conversation that I was having with my apologetic *wingman*.

"I'm Steven, it's great to meet you and here's my card," he said. "If you haven't heard of us, we're EcoGlobalSecuritySystems and we're down in Mountain View. We're a green military defense contractor. Our mission is to build sustainable weapons systems that can annihilate hundreds of thousands of people while still protecting wildlife and minimizing our carbon footprint.

"When we began, we were fresh out of Stanford and idealistic. It was 2003, the invasion of Iraq was underway, and we were immediately concerned about how *green* the war would be. *Can't we have a war that's great for the environment?* we asked ourselves. And out of that vision sprang our enterprise. We put our heads together, formulated a business plan, collected some venture capital, hired a lot of smart people, and threw a bunch of equations onto a whiteboard. At that point, we were thoroughly inspired.

"Unfortunately, the Bush administration doesn't see a role for environmental protection in the war on terror. And just a few months ago, we were disappointed to learn that the Obama campaign isn't giving consideration to us either. So, while it's terrible, we've recently decided to supply our technology to questionable clients. Contrary to all of our allegiances since birth and naturalization, we're now doing business with the Taliban, Al Qaeda, and a portfolio of smaller terrorist organizations. For better or worse, we're the only military defense contractor in the United States that does business with anti-American military forces and radical extremists. And to be honest with you, I'm only somewhat consoled by the fact that we're going public on the NASDAQ in mid-November."

At that point, I was a little dumbfounded. But as I was trying to manufacture an obligatory response, a woman standing behind us thankfully relieved me of the burden.

"Hi, I'm Joan, and I couldn't help but overhear your discussion about the environment," she said. "I work for OceanicEcoRanchingProducts and here's my card. You'll see that my office is on Eddy by Leavenworth, surrounded by bums and cripples who keep choking on their own vomit and dying in their own trash. But our home office is in Iceland, which is great because it's not very ethnic over there.

"Anyway, by exploiting pathetic labor from shithole countries, my company manufactures harpoons made of recycled and recyclable materials. Our mission is to make the slaughtering of whales not just financially practical, but also environmentally responsible. But anyway, we're finding that our revenue is still holding steady, despite this recession caused by Gypsies and sexual deviants."

And that was when I gathered my belongings and said goodbye to my friends and co-workers. But while heading home on the second of two trains, my attention was drawn back toward San Francisco, now well beyond the window, and my business cards collected at the event.

Could you believe that guy Steven? He was undermining national security and endangering the remainder of the world, just for a cheap buck.

But then there was Joan. There was Joan.

After eating breakfast on Saturday morning, I decided to give her a call, hoping that she might be free.

2. The Great Recession

I'm glad that my psychiatrist takes my credit card. Things are getting depressing. And if you're still basking in a fading glow of whatever hope that keeps you together, I don't mean to bring you down. But I do need to warn my friends and notify my acquaintances about the inevitable.

In a matter of months, your currency will be worth nothing. You'll go to the corner store to buy a newspaper and an energy drink and the man behind the counter will tell you: "I'm sorry. This note is from the Department of the Treasury. It is no good here." And he will go on: "If you want to buy this newspaper and this energy drink, you will have to give me your firstborn child." And, after putting a price on your love and subtracting it by your best cost estimate of gratification, you will cry. But he will take pity on you. "Or, perhaps, I could let you compensate me in gold," he will say.

Of course, there will still be love and friendship, kitty cats and puppy dogs. There will be November days in the high 70s. But, if you have a social conscience, you'll deny yourself sunshine. On every beautiful but unseasonable day, we bear witness to catastrophic climate change. By going for a walk or buying a cup of frozen yogurt, we deserve condemnation by future generations.

Also, of course, the remaining stint of our own worldly existence won't be pretty either. Now is a good time to plan for catastrophe. Grow a vegetable garden in your bomb shelter. Snap up buckets for hoarding stormwater. Find a good book for the bread line. Seek advice for interstate travel by foot. Anticipate working twice as hard for half as much. Learn to enjoy the company of locusts. Be prepared for tomorrow. I'm telling you, it will arrive prematurely on the day after today.

3. New Reclining Chair

My old reclining chair was recalled by the North Korean Consumer Protection Bureau, so I bought a new one. It cost one hundred dollars, delivery from the Inner Richmond included. I got the chair on Craigslist, much like everything else that I possess: my job, my apartment, my spiritual enlightenment, my reclining chair, etc.

After no successes in the "missed connections" and "casual encounters" sections of Craigslist, I finally went to the "furniture" section and quickly found what I was looking for. So, now I have my chair. But unfortunately, now there's a woman at my bus stop who should acknowledge me, but doesn't. That, and tomorrow I'm meeting three people in a public restroom without the benefit of lights.

My misfortune doesn't end there. Now that I have a chair again, there's nothing good on television. My favorite TV show, C-Span's "Prime Minister's Questions" went immediately downhill after they shuffled off my favorite character, Tony Blair. And on Comedy Central, they're not showing rebroadcasts of Jon Stewart.

I can't watch Jon Stewart on Monday and Wednesday nights, because those nights I have miniature golf endurance training. And I can't watch him on Tuesday and Thursday nights, because those nights I help my cousin with his court-ordered paperwork for being a sexual predator. I do it because I'm nice and he's family. Also, he pays me back in crystal methamphetamine and 7-Eleven microwavable burritos.

4. A Day Surrendered to Consultation

It had been a difficult time both personally and professionally, so I was eager to leave the apartment to gather with my co-workers for a daylong workshop. And although my girlfriend expressed little interest when I opened the door and said goodbye, everyone at work seemed relieved to see each other given events in the news.

And our instructors for the day, Stream of Consciousness Consulting, started the day off with some worthwhile exercises:

ICE BREAKERS

Stream of Consciousness Consulting

1. Share with everyone your name, age, income, nationality, religious beliefs, political affiliations, marital status, sexual orientation, gender identity, and any disabilities that you might have.

2. Identify the person in the office whom you are
    least attracted to. Tell them to their face why
    you would never have sex with them.
3. In front of the full group, say two bad things
    about your race.
4. In small groups, answer the following questions:
    Does your organization have a mission
    statement? What is it? Would you be willing to
    die for it? Would you be willing to kill for it?

Afterward, we all took a break to enjoy water at room
temperature, and when we reconvened, our consultants
led us into the second event. "There are six types of
office workers, and you probably work with all of
them," the lead consultant began. "They are: busy bees,
wanderers, patriarchs, prostitutes, schizophrenics and
thieves. All are equally important to a successful
organization," he explained. And at that juncture we
were encouraged to take notes:

THE SIX TYPES OF OFFICE WORKERS
Stream of Consciousness Consulting

1. **Busy bees** – Busy bees help in several ways by
    seeing projects through to completion and by

preparing themselves for upcoming assignments. Busy bees are very important.

2. **Wanderers** – Wanderers break down organizational silos by drifting into areas of the office where they do not belong. Invariably, they will end up eating their lunches at the loading dock.

3. **Patriarchs** – Patriarchs know everything because they are men, not women, and because they are usually white. Knowing they would be useless under a better economic system, patriarchs sign the paychecks of the employees.

4. **Prostitutes** – Prostitutes have sex with other people for money.

5. **Schizophrenics** – Schizophrenics keep the office tidy by destroying files they falsely perceive to be about themselves. Schizophrenics can also yell at demons in the office that others may not see.

6. **Thieves** – Thieves may steal boxes of paper clips or embezzle millions of dollars, but they are always important. Thieves help other employees feel better about their own transgressions and moral standing. Every organization should have at least one thief.

More notes of importance were taken throughout the day, and the remainder of the session was so informative that we all agreed to stay late. So, afterward, I got home using the first ridesharing service in the history of the world. And pleased with my entire experience, I awarded my driver perfect scores in all of the categories that are still used to measure driver performance: ✓ Safe driving, ✓ Warm car, ✓ Minimal homophobic conversation, ✓ Reluctance to join a union.

However, when I got inside, I found my girlfriend at the top of the staircase with one of her boots severely mangled. And she gave me an ultimatum. "It's either the dog or me," my woman said.

So, I did what any other man would do.

I put my dog to sleep and repaired my relationship.

5. In Accepting This Award

[Begin speech]

In accepting this award for 2008 White Man of the Year, I would like to give thanks to my wife, who never lets her Xanax addiction get in the way of her tennis game. To my definitively prettier mistress, who never ties her hush money to the rate of inflation. To my wonderful children, who are at boarding school somewhere. To my parents – my father, a truck driver, and my mother, a librarian – both of whom I have obviously outperformed.

I believe deeply in this charity and I have a lot of money, so I had little hesitation or difficulty in writing this check. The work that you do on behalf of children, or the environment, or whatever – I truly find it to be vitally important.

But by no means, however, will this be my only photo opportunity for the year. In hospital rooms, I push people with terminal diseases to live their best lives. In emergency shelters, I help victims of natural disasters express gratitude for everything they used to have. And when stalled in city traffic, I yell at homeless people to get jobs. Simply put, I am the most considerate person in the world.

And so, as I add this honor to the fourth paragraph of my online biography, I plead to be recognized not for my tax evasion, my insider trading, my retaliation against whistleblowers, my subversion of organized labor, my discriminatory hiring and lending practices, my profiteering from the gross exploitation of natural resources, my harassment of vulnerable people through the legal system, nor my shoveling of untraceable campaign contributions to politicians obliged to do the bidding of my industry, but rather, for why we're here tonight:

My philanthropy.

6. A Banner Night for Marriage Inequality

[Sacramento Bee – November 5, 2008]

On a night that saw the election of the country's first Black president, expanded majorities for Democrats in Congress, and the triumph of key progressive initiatives by way of the ballot box, stood one outlying result: the victory of California Proposition 8, banning same-sex marriage in the state. Today, California Secretary of State Debra Bowen acknowledged its passage by an apparent margin of 52% to 48%. Exit polls explain why:

Of voters who know the creator to be capable of nothing but love, laughter and justice – reluctant to assign his children a sexual orientation that could get them killed, persecuted, or bullied in the name of his most celebrated son – the proposition failed (12% to 88%).

However, among voters who believe that God enjoys nothing more than a brutal series of cruel jokes, including the placement of his gay and lesbian children onto Earth to live in self-hatred and fear, the proposition passed overwhelmingly (95% to 5%). Additionally, voters who love Jesus, but not what he said, approved of the proposal (92% to 8%).

Men favored the proposition (59% to 41%), as did real men (75% to 25%), as did real men destined to live the remainder of their lives alone (91% to 9%). Of married men who can't understand why single women are turned off by their wedding rings, the proposal was successful (58% to 42%).

Men thrice divorced, having left wives diagnosed with cancer, approved of the marriage restriction (81% to 19%).

Of married heterosexual couples with negotiated prenuptial agreements, the proposal was approved (51% to 49%). However, among gay and lesbian caretakers denied the right to be bedside for the deaths of their loving partners, the proposal was turned down (1% to 99%).

After the victory, Yes on 8 campaign manager Pat Springwell addressed a celebratory ballroom of supporters. "Tonight was a great night for teaching our children to hate other people," said Springwell. "Going forward, I hope we will be able to deny civil rights other marginalized groups."

7. A Radical Shift in Company Culture

For the better part of a year, I had the misfortune to work downtown at Predatory Lending Services, Inc. It was terrible. Among our many humiliations as employees, to enter the locked restrooms, we had to tell our supervisors if we needed to go "pee pee" or "poo poo." And once inside, there was a posted sign that read:

> Washing your hands exhausts
> 20 seconds of company time

The place was so bad, it was listed among the *Worst Places in the Bay Area to Work 2008* by the *San Francisco Business Times*, even making it into the top five: 5) Silicon Valley Community Foundation, 4) Predatory Lending Services, 3) Honey Bucket Portable Toilets and Hotels, 2) O'Farrell Pornographic Theater–Ejaculate Rag Division, and 1) Facebook.

However, when our company was acquired by a new partnership in December 2008, improvements were made across the board. And two weeks after the acquisition, a memo was distributed by our new leadership team that gave encouragement to many. It read:

We are committed to addressing
the issue of workplace diversity

It brought my only Black co-worker, Gladys Robinson, to tears. "They told us we were free, but we weren't free," she said. "They told us we could vote, but we couldn't vote. And in Tulsa, Oklahoma in 1921, they burned our center of finance to the ground.

"But tonight, I can tell everyone who has struggled so hard for justice – including my own elders – that I am employed by a company that is committed to addressing the issue of workplace diversity. First, the election of a Black president. But now this. Doctor King is smiling in heaven, with the view from his promised mountaintop now easy for everyone to see."

8. Story Eight of Twelve

In 2008, you will dream of making it in Hollywood, finishing a triathlon, buying a house with a two car garage, and bringing children into the world. But five years later, you will be performing meaningless tasks under fluorescent lights, being sad and sedentary, arguing with negligent roommates, staying perpetually single, and empathizing with much of the following scenario:

It begins on a Saturday night, when you've already lost 15% of your paycheck to the middle shelf at the club. And you will remain at the bar throughout a million iterations of the same song, until the lady next to you will give up on her night and settle on you by default. She will be your only source of affection for your foreseeable future.

Of course, upon the first sight of you on Sunday morning, the poor woman will rush to the kitchen to take the morning-after pill. And, while trying to put that slight out of mind on your dejected walk home, you will wonder why no one sells hash browns in your whole goddamn municipality.

Sunday afternoon will follow, when your favorite NFL team will be mathematically eliminated from reaching the playoffs. So, of course, you will seek solace in Downton Abbey at night, despite being eternally perplexed as to why PBS would air a show much about nightmarish labor on the very night before everyone has to return to it themselves.

Fortunately, however, you will receive good sleep thanks to exhaustion. But two hours into the new morning you will be greeted by the biggest asshole in the office. "Happy Monday!" the asshole will say. So, you will put your headphones on to drown out his bullshit, and their bullshit, and all of the bullshit surrounding you. But with the volume up too high, you will never know the answer to the question: *Is my farting audible?*

Yet, regardless of that uncertainty, your headphones will remain your most cherished possession (second only to your grandfather's salad fork that belonged to him during a war). However, on Tuesday, you will be required to put them aside when two of your co-workers will choose you to resolve a few of their arguments.

Co-worker #1 will argue that Obama was born in Sweden. Co-worker #2 will argue that the 1989 Loma Prieta earthquake was an inside job. Co-worker #1 will argue that everybody with brown eyes is here illegally. Co-worker #2 will argue that everybody has a birthright to unlimited tofu. Co-worker #1 will argue that elderly bisexuals are plotting to confiscate his assault rifles. Co-worker #2 will argue that a United Nations flag should wave at half-mast whenever a member of a mime troupe dies. Co-worker #1 will argue that vaccines are a way for governments to pacify their own people. And Co-worker #2 will argue that vaccines are a way for governments to pacify their own people.

But, wise enough not to involve yourself in the disputes, you will drop to the floor and pretend to be unconscious. And so, the two belligerents will move on to the intern, cornering that sad bastard to settle their idiotic quarrels.

However, next up will be Wednesday – your third consecutive day of showing up! And on that day you will attend the "Wednesday Wellness Workshop" sponsored by your employer, but will be surprised by the advice of the guest psychologist. "To alleviate workplace stress," the psychologist will say, "you should lock yourself in a bathroom, curl into the fetal position, and cry like a baby."

Of course, you will take the advice, but 378 Thursdays later it will prove to be entirely unnecessary. Sending you home indefinitely, your boss will give you a laptop and four bottles of hand sanitizer. And as the subsequent months go by, more than seven million will die around the world, but you will be able to fold laundry between meetings.

And there will be other perks. Situated at home, your hands will stop shuffling, your shoulders will stop tightening, your heart will stop racing, and your mind will stop spinning. And while enjoying Casual Fridays within the confines of your apartment, you will constantly distract your cats from their responsibilities, until reaching into your refrigerator for a Happy Hour that is partially deserved.

9. Counterproductive Spiritual Quest

With enough cash on hand, I would've ventured to the upper reaches of the Himalayas to find the answers. But in an effort to find inner peace on the cheap, I recently scaled Mount Diablo instead. My journey began in the paid parking lot (base camp) on Saturday at 2:00 and I reached the summit at 2:05. And when I got to the top, I found a wise man in his 90s sitting beneath a tree.

And he instantly knew what I was there for. "You want my help in discerning your purpose," he said. "But I need to be honest with you: the enlightenment of mankind has always been unprofitable, so instead, now I'm buying undervalued assets in turbulent financial markets. And when I looked ten minutes ago, the S&P was twelve points off in after-close trading. It's a direct result of yesterday's correction in Shanghai. So you won't find me greeting the sun, playing my flute, or pretending that meditation has a purpose anymore. And I had to euthanize all of the birds on my shoulders, but when the world rebounds I'll be hosting parties on a boat.

"But you seem like an alright guy. Maybe I can help you out," he continued. "Do you believe in God?" he asked.

"Yes," I replied.

"Have you accepted Jesus Christ as your personal savior?" he asked.

"No, not really," I said. "I have questions that would probably lead to stipulations."

"I see," he said. "Let's give you someone's cell. It belongs to Father Bob Nastanovich of Our Lady of Good Times. No relation to the esteemed equestrian on backup vocals and drums. He's down the hill in Walnut Creek. A solid guy. It's funny – he was nearly kicked out of seminary for selling drugs. Fortunately, the Vatican has its own way of overlooking things, but yes, good luck."

So, after a friendly goodbye, I descended from Mount Diablo and drove back into Walnut Creek. I stopped at the Chipotle downtown, ate a tostada even though it wasn't on the menu, and placed a call with the priest.

He said he was free and gave me a general direction to his cathedral.

Finding the corresponding exact location proved to be easy, as was putting on my guest badge, but I took several wrong turns trying to find the father's corner office. And when I finally saw him, he was wearing a green visor and shuffling a deck of cards by himself, eager to get to the point of my visit. "What are you doing here?" he asked. "What's your thing?"

I thought there was no harm in confiding. "I'm trying to discern my purpose," I said.

He did not respond, but I proceeded anyway.

"I want to benefit humanity through my art," I said. "That's why I formed a band a few months ago. So far, we've only performed covers for friends, but I can already sense that we are harnessing God's love and bringing joy to a world that needs it.

"And, although it's not everyone's assignment, I think I'd be a good father," I went on. "Regardless of whatever resources they might consume, whatever waste they might produce, or whatever impact they might have on the climate, children can lead worthwhile lives by making people in society feel loved."

Again, I did not receive a response, but still felt compelled to continue.

"Meanwhile – and I hope I'm not getting ahead of myself – but I'm pretty sure that I've met *the one*. Six months ago, the two of us were at the dog park talking about the weather. But since then, we've revealed to each other our biggest dreams and deepest fears. And so I'm also seeking another confirmation: *Is she God's match for me?*"

Feeling better, I stopped, but the priest glared at me before he responded.

"Well," he said. "First off – an all knowing God is aware of your shitty band and every shitty band in the Bay Area. There are hundreds of them. You may not have to listen to all of them, but God does. This creative project that you aren't shutting up about is destined to fail. So, if you want to do anything with your life, put away childish things and get practical. God wants all of his children to observe Lent and have a good grasp of Microsoft Office Suite. Guessing from your presumed age and occupation, I'm assuming you have some command of MS Word and MS Excel. You're probably satisfactory in the eyes of God, so you don't need to get carried away, Sir Paul McCartney.

"Secondly," he said, "dog owners visit dog parks out of desperation for *human* companionship, not dog companionship. And I speak from personal experience. Not too long ago, I made a big mistake with a woman from a dog park. And let me tell you, I should have abided by the Human Resources Policy Manual of the Roman Catholic Church, because this woman wasn't worth it. And let me tell you something. Listen to me. Women with bags of dog shit will always exude kindness –

And that's why you're bound to overlook the dog shit in their hands."

He looked at his phone twice, and then spoke again.

"We were together in a month with 31 days and she left me for an urban planner with a golden retriever. And as if breaking my heart wasn't enough, I had to see her with that man all of the time. And do you know what was worse than their public displays of affection?" he asked.

"It was their private displays of affection," he said.

And then, capable of nothing but staring outside, the father became fixated on a pallet of communion wafers awaiting a forklift. And it took an alarm on his phone for his preoccupation to end.

"Holy shit!" he shouted. "It's five o'clock and I need to get the hell out of here. My shift is over. Here's my card. I've got a six o'clock date that I need to find on Capp Street. Tonight we're seeing a film in the Tenderloin. It's about people who fuck each other."

But before leaving, the father reached into his desk and handed me a scrap of paper. "Here's a ticket for tomorrow's Mass," he said. "You'll have the best seat in the house for glancing at the crucifix." So, after taking the ticket, I followed him to his sports car and thanked him for his time.

But at home, I felt lost again, and without high expectations for the day to come. So I dusted the interior of my refrigerator and drank two and a half beers – unprepared, however, for what was on my horizon. Because upon arrival at the cathedral on Sunday morning, I became wholly immersed in the unconditional love of Jesus Christ. And the experience was beautiful and transformative, until I saw some bitch in my seat (Row A, Seat 4), who I immediately had removed.

In her defense, however, I soon discovered why she wanted a front row seat. In his Mass, Father Nastanovich had amazing things to say about hope, faith, charity, doubling down on a soft 17, remembering Mary as a 9, but a Bethlehem 10, and navigating life in general. He also kept returning to a message, telling his parishioners: "Whenever you do something wrong, make an excuse for yourself. Just say: <u>I am but a vessel of God</u>.

"Whenever you walk by a lemonade stand without making a purchase, whenever you turn off your television at the first sight of human suffering, whenever you hit a pedestrian and speed off, just remember to say: <u>I am but a vessel of God</u>."

And the liturgy made the crowd go completely wild. So, after the father's final encore, I rushed to the front to get his autograph, as did droves of other passionate fans. But I wasn't successful in my efforts, and went home without even speaking to anyone.

Nevertheless, even without any validation from others, I awoke on Monday morning with an entirely new purpose and direction in life. So, I ate breakfast, took a shower, skipped work, and sold my guitar and two grams of PCP to a high school freshman in Atherton. I arrived at a total of $1,150 ($150 for the guitar and $500 for each gram) – easily afforded with his weekly allowance of $5,000 in equities and treasury bonds. But I walked away feeling guilty for overcharging him, or at least I did, until I recalled the father's message: <u>I am but a vessel of God</u>.

But I wasn't done. With my afternoon free, I got high on PCP myself, and decided to call the prospective mother of my children to propose marriage. However, I also attempted to go big with an addendum: reserving a right to see a prostitute every twelve nights leading up to the rehearsal dinner. But, of course, both requests were refused, just as my right mind would have forewarned. Instead, on the same extended weekend when my hopes for artistic expression were vanquished, so too were my hopes for family life. But later into the night, with a special edition of *Maxim* in one hand and the other hand getting busy, I shed responsibility and recalled the father's message: <u>I am but a vessel of God</u>!

10. A Funeral Not to be Missed

They came through Newark, LaGuardia, JFK, Port Authority, Penn Station and Grand Central. Or by the R Train, the Battery Tunnel, the LIE or the BQE. But it was all for the same purpose: to pay respects to a young man who died too soon. And they left flowers by a tombstone that read:

HERE LIES OUR BELOVED
BENJAMIN WALLER
(1976 – 2008)

DIED VALIANTLY, RIOTING WHILE
INTOXICATED AFTER THE NEW YORK
GIANTS WON SUPER BOWL XLII

And sure, there were VIPs in attendance: the local councilman, who would go on to lose a bid for Congress on his platform of taxing text messages and improving conditions for prisoners; the nihilistic neighborhood video store clerk, who would go on to popularize a bumper sticker reading NO LIVES MATTER; and the cheapest guru in the borough, who would go on to resign from the trade and become the greatest high school football coach in the history of Vermont.

But the four most important people in attendance were Ben's fiancé Laura, Ben's brother Jason, and Ben's two parents. And Laura was the first to speak.

"Thank you for being here today, but of course, we wanted to be together for the wedding instead of this," she said. "And although Ben and I were both looking forward to you throwing rice at our car, our real joy would have been in having children for you adore – at birthdays, recitals, graduations, and more. But we all know why we're here.

Ben was intense. And although he was never abusive, his idea for proposing to me was to yell at me when I was sleeping. But I couldn't say no, because I loved him, and I know that all of you loved him too."

Jason followed.

"Thank you for being here today, it really means so much to our family," he said.

"As you all know, my brother was passionate about so many things – but man did he love sports and man did he hate authority! At Shea, he would remain seated for the national anthem but hold his hand over his heart for *Take Me Out to the Ballgame.* And in college, he majored in American Studies, but had an Anti-American Studies minor.

And so, when Ben threw those trash cans through the windows of that police station, it wasn't just about his love for the Giants. Instead, it was also about the world that he wanted for his children."

And that was how Ben was remembered. The crowd dissipated, and Laura and Jason left together. The councilman had dinner with a mob boss in New Jersey. The clerk crammed for his midterms at art school. And the guru packed his bags for the next day's Ethan Allen Express. But Ben's parents remained, gazing at their son's grave.

But they didn't express an ounce of grief, because they were too overwhelmed with pride.

"We raised him right, didn't we?" asked Ben's father rhetorically.

And Ben's mother concurred.

"We most certainly did," she said. "But we better give Coughlin another contract extension for any chance at a serious dynasty."

11. Blessing of the I-5 Corridor

After accruing my first 40 hours of vacation time from my job at the hippest North American corporate record store, I decided to visit some family in Washington State for Christmas: my cousin Harry and his daughter Stacey. They are the two most interesting people known to me.

Harry was born in Tacoma and now lives in Seattle. And during the entirety of the U.S. invasion of Grenada – from the beginning of the operation (October 25, 1983) to Victory Over Grenada Day (October 29, 1983) – he ran a rest and relaxation station for GI's returning from the island. The station, located in central Beirut, was once visited by Laurence Tureaud (then widely known as Mr. T) and by First Lady Nancy Reagan (with direction from the U.S. Department of Astrology and superficial consultation with the U.S. Department of Defense).

But two years later, Harry was dishonorably discharged from the service for the off-the-books offense of requesting the Clash on Armed Forces Radio. So, for the next twelve years, he taught Portuguese literature at

North Seattle Community College, until becoming sick of the Portuguese language and people.

Microsoft followed, where he worked on the research and development team for spinning cursors, but after ten years the company found an undocumented worker to perform his job for three quarters of his salary.

Understandably, Harry got bitter, but he didn't succumb to nationalism. When speaking with me, he blamed immigration not for costing him a job, but rather, for making it difficult to excel at pick-up games of soccer during his lengthy unemployment.

But eventually, good luck arrived for my cousin, albeit in disguise. After returning quickly from a game on a rainy Thursday in August, he encountered his wife and best friend together in bed. And, out of raw instinct, he did something understandable: he asked them to complete their sexual activities elsewhere so that he could take a nap.

And as a result, on the following well-rested Friday, the Washington State Ferries system hired him as a captain without demanding relevant experience, right on the spot.

Today, Harry continues to play soccer, and aspires to play women's basketball. He owns eight jerseys of his favorite WNBA players and sits courtside for the Seattle Storm. And privately, he expresses a desire to play women's basketball professionally, but believes that as a man, his opportunities in a female-dominated enterprise are limited without most institutional privileges typically afforded by the patriarchy. And sadly, until a few years ago, Harry tried to live vicariously through his daughter Stacey, hoping she would live out his own ambitions in the arena of women's athletics.

But Stacey has other interests. Always buried in blueprints, she currently studies civil engineering at the Evergreen State College. Last semester, she sailed through "Reinforced Concrete for People's Liberation 401" and offered an excellent argument in her term paper:

"I think we should round up problematic people and persuade them by force to rebuild roads south of here. The roads will require porous asphalt, with a high percentage of air voids, allowing most water to pass through and infiltrate the subsoil. Only then will supply

routes out of Portland be prepared for regiments of
Antifa bicycles."

Her class loved it. And in Stacey's written evaluation
(in Evergreen's standard format of a haiku), her
professor and co-equal encouraged her to sell the whole
paper as a zine in the most popular coffee shop in
downtown Olympia. She did – and in only ten days, it
was bought up by the shop's clientele of poets,
transients, and state employees.

The coffee shop was also where Stacey found my
Christmas gift: a bootleg spoken-word cassette of
Governor Christine Gregoire performing live in front
of a joint session of the Washington State Legislature. I
was deeply appreciative of the present, and she
expressed sincere appreciation for my present: an image
I downloaded of Bill Ayres sitting on a bench in
downtown Chicago with a handicapped dog.

But sadly, Sunday came too quickly, as it always does.
And on that day, I suffered the brutal reminder that
returning flights are rarely enjoyable. So, when my
flight attendants were finally done boring the entire
plane with their totally rehearsed instructions on how
to stay alive, I immediately regretted putting airports

into my plan for the day. But fortunately, I still had Stacey's gift on hand. And so, from cruising altitude to baggage claim, I kept rewinding to the governor's comments about amending the Growth Management Act, which resulted in cathartic sobbing every time.

But Stacey's generosity didn't end with the tape. When I got home to the lobby of my apartment building, I saw nine packages addressed to me, accompanied by a card reading:

Dear Forrest,
In each of these repurposed boxes you will find a compostable doll, made by consensus in an egalitarian community where trees are listened to and not ignored. There are nine in total – each representing each day that you graciously spent with us.
Love, Stacey

So, on Monday morning, after a two-hour conference call about where to file Neko Case after her most recent album, I did the most important thing that I would do all year: I requested vacation time to return for the week of June 29, 2009 – six months away.

12. Keeping in Touch With the Nearly Rehabilitated

When I meet people for the first time, I mention that I wear running shoes for everyday use, that I won a sixth grade vice presidential election cleanly, but decisively, and that I witnessed the first hat trick in San Jose Sharks history. I do not tell them about my stay in a psychiatric hospital.

But everything got underway on the night of Easter Sunday 2008, when I offered my first sincere prayer to the Lord. And although much was revealed through the unanticipated success of the act, in confusion, I came to believe that Jesus had anointed me to be his administrative assistant. So, in this assumed capacity, I reserved a banquet room at the Olive Garden in the Stonestown Galleria for a private dinner for Jesus and a new round of disciples. But of course, no one showed up. That's why I committed myself to Alta Bates Herrick Hospital in Berkeley, knowing that I needed help. And although I would never recommend being hospitalized for pleasure, I did meet four good friends during my time there. And when the pandemic subsided, I took one day to revisit all of them. They were Peter Spencer, Samantha Wilcox, Floyd Jefferson, and Jack Weatherly.

PETER SPENCER

My first roommate at Herrick was Peter Spencer. Peter moved from the Midwest to San Francisco to study advertising at the Academy of Art University – the only course of study the university offers. And, as is customary at the university, he received his diploma three days later, when his check for tuition cleared the bank.

However, Peter's life soon became unmanageable. In March of 2008, he reported a mental inability to recycle, telling his admitting staff that Satan was commanding him not to.

"THEY SHOULD BE ABLE TO SORT IT AT THE FACILITY," the master of darkness was telling Peter, with no bearing on the truth.

"THEY SHOULD BE ABLE TO SORT IT AT THE FACILITY," five thousand demons were screaming in Peter's head.

And, although Peter found peace with the right medication, one week prior to his discharge his parents told him to never return home. And it was impossible for me to console him after the call. "I have no one, Forrest," he told me. "I don't have anyone anymore, and there's nowhere in this place for me to die."

However, instead of allowing himself to fall by the wayside, Peter put together an exceptional life for himself. And today, from a three bedroom house shared with his wife and three children, he works remotely for the City of San Leandro as the *idea man* behind its public service advertisements. And furthermore, for his commendable accomplishments in raising a harmonious family while taking 1200 milligrams of Lithium every day, he was even once featured on the cover of *Bipolar Dad Magazine.*

Meanwhile, Peter's professional work has also seen publication – in both the *Journal of Public Service Advertisement* and *Public Service Advertisement Today.* However, some critics believe that too many resentments from his psychological ordeals are reflected in his portfolio, drawing particular attention to:

Signs on every trash can reading –

DON'T LITTER
THIS IS FUCKING SAN LEANDRO

A billboard by Highway 880 –

DON'T FUCK WITH THE SAN LEANDRO
POLICE DEPARTMENT

IF YOU FUCK WITH THEM,
THEY WILL FUCK YOUR SHIT UP

Posters at the library –

MUST SAN LEANDRO TEACHERS
DO EVERYTHING FOR YOU AND
YOUR STUPID CHILDREN?

TEACH YOUR FUCKING
KIDS HOW TO READ!

**And perhaps one worth conceding, this message on
a bus shelter on East 14th Street –**

DON'T BE A FUCKING LUNATIC
GET YOUR SHIT TOGETHER

Nevertheless, I remain a big fan of Peter's work, and I always enjoy seeing it in person. So, when he told me about a truly great Starbucks in his city, I immediately knew that it would be the perfect place to meet. However, as I noted to Peter, it was my first time at a Starbucks since 1999, when I camped out overnight for the autobiography of Howard Schultz.

But since then, I had forgotten a lot about the entity. In particular, when I inquired into the whereabouts of the tip jars, the barista I spoke to laughed. "No need to tip at this store, sir," he said. "All Starbucks employees have the perk of being able to buy shares of the Starbucks Corporation with our own wealth."

And upon that understanding, I took a third straw after failing to commit to the first two, and felt comfortable choosing a seat that spoke to me. Peter showed up not long afterward. "This seat speaks to me too," he agreed.

However, from the outset, Peter and I knew that our time was limited. His second favorite child had a kickball quarterfinal and was an indispensable element to the success of the team. But we still managed to cover important territory: how we weren't praying for the health of our 45th president, how we were viewing

our IRA balances daily (something completely
premature given our income and age), and how our
small children had already surpassed us in intelligence.
However, the latter raised an additional financial
concern for Peter. "Every parent worries about the
expenses of college and the substance abuse treatment
that follows," he said. And with that, he told me to give
his regards to Samantha Wilcox, a mutual crush from
the hospital, whom I saw next.

SAMANTHA WILCOX

I caught up with Samantha in Berkeley at Cafe
Indifference, a quirky restaurant where, before
ordering, patrons are encouraged to tell the waitstaff
what they are indifferent to. Going first, Samantha
expressed her indifference to the Golden Globe Awards
and asked for their Steven Spielberg soup. I followed by
expressing my indifference to the Winter Olympics and
the College World Series, and asked for their David
Brooks salad.

I first got to know Samantha in May of 2008, the
month of her involuntary admission. And when she was
brought through the doors, she was wearing black jeans
and black Chuck Taylor shoes, with a sheet reading

Smash the State safety pinned to the back of her black hooded sweatshirt. But despite her appearance, she wasn't an anarchist. Her contempt for agents of public safety was specific to firefighters. She had no problems with the police.

"WHO HAS THE AUDACITY TO EXTINGUISH A FIRE?" Samantha asked Peter and I one night in explaining her views. "A fire is a living organism, just like a basket, or car insurance. Meanwhile, police officers are doing what they're supposed to do – they enforce laws enacted by representatives in governmental bodies," she said. "These representatives are duly elected though free, fair and frequent elections. Meanwhile, firefighters get shittier and shittier as the seasons change. Last year, they came into Gilman propagating THE LIE OF MAXIMUM CAPACITY. How many people will they count until they have no one left to count?

"And it's always the same: *We're from the fire department and we're here to help* or *We're from the fire department and we're looking out for you.* But we shouldn't let firefighters interrupt death with their violent preservation of life. And firefighters keep protecting us from danger, which should make them downright ashamed of themselves.

"And you can read the New Testament. You can read the Magna Carta. You can read the preamble to the Constitution. You can read the United Nations Universal Declaration of Human Rights, and I'll guarantee you this: you won't find the phrase *fire department* anywhere. Everyone knows that 90% of firefighting is bullshit and the other 10% could be done by kids."

It was quite a statement. But I didn't argue with the assertion (or any of her others), and I quickly became her boyfriend because of my restraint. And in less than four weeks, Samantha and I were sharing each other's prescribed medications, making out underneath a broken air hockey table, and reading to each other in a corner of the common area. But our relationship fell apart on one particularly difficult night, when a local news item finally forced a divide.

"Look at this astonishing article on page two of the *Berkeley Daily Hyperbolic Garbage!*" Samantha exclaimed to me. "It says that a serial arsonist is unjustly being denied participation in a middle school career day event!"

Needless to say, Samantha was incensed at the school. But my outrage was more muted, and it showed. So a reprisal followed. With only modest warning, she attacked me with a plastic fork, shouting "THIS MUST REMIND YOU OF YOUR GREATEST WET DREAM" between every other swing.

But she didn't know me when I was fourteen, so the experience still keeps me wondering. And worrying.

How did she know?

FLOYD JEFFERSON

I was still too afraid to ask, so with two more visits left, I asked the cashier for directions to my third destination: Improved Mission Cupcakes in San Francisco. It was recommended by my friend, Floyd Jefferson, a former Herrick patient and former linebacker for the University of California Golden Bears.

She glowed. "I love Improved Cupcakes!" she said. "It's a great place for uninteresting people and their boring experiences! Just take an Uber from Downtown Berkeley BART to 16th & Mission BART," she said. "You'll have a great time."

I certainly did, but I crossed the bay too early, giving me three hours to kill in the city. But with time on my hands downtown, I discovered a chain bookstore for middle class heterosexual Caucasians, where I lost myself in conventional thought.

But not lost enough to forget about Floyd, who had been holding our place in line for the majority of the morning and the entirety of the afternoon. But, for him, the wait was worth everything when he finally shook hands with the hostess, whom he was so eager to meet.

"It's two of us for dinner," he said to her cheerfully.

But she laughed at him, forcing Floyd to be firm.

"*We have reservations*," he said.

"Oh, then my apologies," she said. "Right this way, sir."

In the hospital, if you couldn't finish your meal, you gave it to Floyd. Floyd was 6'1" and 240 pounds, and his first season with the Bears was on its unsuccessful 2001 team – a team that went 1-10 under Tom Holmoe. Head Coach Jeff Tedford took over the next year, and Floyd became a favorite of Tedford and the rest of the Bears coaching staff.

But in the hospital, Floyd would eat his meals with his headphones on, always giving his full attention to what he was listening to. And one morning, I was surprised to see him enjoying a CD by the former Olympia-based group Bikini Kill.

The group, which formed in 1990, was central to the establishment of third wave feminism and the "riot grrl" movement – rarely associated with college football. However, as I learned as we got to know each other, Bikini Kill was Floyd's favorite band. "Their shit always gets me pumped," he told me.

And in 2002, it showed on the field. Tedford turned Cal Football around dramatically, and Floyd was a key figure in its success. Cal finished 7-5 and would have gone to a bowl game that year had it not been for academic infractions. I remember the season very well, because during it, the Bears broke a 19-game losing streak against Washington, the school that I went to. Floyd had a great game against us and was named All-Conference that year. *"It was because I was listening to Pussy Whipped before each game,"* he told me.

Floyd even made good use of Bikini Kill to help win the 2002 Big Game against Stanford. With a big lead going into the second half, Tedford asked Floyd to give the game's halftime speech. And the primary source of Floyd's material was perceptible:

"Hey girlfriends," he began. "I've got a proposition and it goes something like this: I dare you to do what you want. I dare you to be who you will. I dare you to cry right out loud. Before Carter reaches, take him down! And when Eklund drops back, hit that asshole!

"And gentlemen, during the first half we won our races and scored our points. And in the second half, we're taking our poetry to the photocopier. It's almost as if we're taking the stage at the Capitol Theater. Front stage. This is for the axe. This is for the sexy leopard print headbands worn well by our defensive line. This is for our pride, and the pride of our school. I believe in the radical possibilities of pleasure. I believe in the radical possibilities of this team. We're one half away from winning the Big Game, so let's go out there and beat the shit out of those motherfuckers!"

The speech obviously worked. Cal beat Stanford 30 to 7, and after a seven-year losing streak, the axe was returned to Berkeley. In Herrick, I had a good time talking to Floyd about the game, and college football generally. In return, he was interested in the music that I was listening to. I introduced him to a lot of bands – including Scottish bands that I hoped would keep him at ease, like Belle and Sebastian, Camera Obscura and The Pastels. Floyd appreciated the recommendations, but was particularly interested in a San Francisco-based group, The Aislers Set, and their second album, *The Last Match*. Floyd kept listening to the song *The Walk* and even made a point of talking to me about it.

"Forrest," he said to me. "I'm listening to *The Walk* and it's making me think about things. Just as Amy described, I've been waking up at three in the afternoon to shower for hours. And then I'll watch porn all alone for the evening, but it never really gets me anywhere except back in the shower. Some see me as a kid with a filthy mind, but they've never seen my sentimental side.

"When I get out of Herrick, I'm going to show them my sentimental side," he said.

True to his word, Floyd delivered on his promise. After he was discharged, KNBR Sports 680 gave him a show with an early morning time slot. But unfortunately, over time many listeners shunned it, dismissing it as *too sentimental.*

The first breaking point was Floyd's broadcast after the 2009 Major League All-Star Game. Reading from a sheet, he said on the air: "Well, Timmy got into a little trouble in the first but had a solid second. But once again, nothing could help the National League."

But then Floyd went off script, and invited the haters to hate.

"However, the best moment was Obama on TV during the bottom of the second," he said. "Apparently, the president wore his White Sox jersey for the first pitch because Michelle told him that he looked cute in it. So, this morning, we'll talk about the All-Star Game and the second half for the Giants, but more importantly, we'll talk about how we feel about the ones we love."

Floyd's revised tagline didn't help, either: "I'm Floyd Jefferson, this is KNBR Sports 680, and I find a lot of things to be endearing."

The criticism kept growing, but he didn't care. After an away game against the Mets, he told his listeners: "Well, Zito had a rough outing again, but let's appreciate him for doing his best. And really, why should the score of the game be important? It puts too much pressure on the players. What's truly important is that the Giants tried, everyone had a good time, and that no one got hurt."

But, as many foresaw, Floyd was fired from KNBR and now makes a living by selling essential oils for schizophrenia. "My broadcasting career is on hiatus," he explained. "Just like Superchunk once was, and like the Korean War will always be."

But after a few cupcakes, Floyd forgot about his setbacks and spoke enthusiastically about his new job – and its celebrated business model. In the model, named the "pyramid model," participants earn their income by recruiting an infinite number of members, who do the same in turn. And, being considerate, Floyd asked me if I wanted in. Needless to say, I told him that I most assuredly did, but that I couldn't sign any paperwork on the spot (I had plans to meet Jack Weatherly). So Floyd hugged me goodbye, but not too affectionately, as we had just agreed to be business partners.

And so, feeling confident about my financial health, I turned my attention to my physical health – imperative after eating too many cupcakes for dinner. So I went to a street vendor and ordered a kale and quinoa salad, along with a Pellegrino and fresh lemon wedge. And believing that an evening stroll through the Tenderloin would be pleasant, I decided to walk to my next destination. But like clockwork, I saw two *techies* walking down the street with bloody clothing, bitching about "armed robbery" and "unprovoked assault." But I rolled my eyes at both of them and made my way through the Stockton Street Tunnel to Chinatown, and on to North Beach from there.

JACK WEATHERLY

To begin to understand Jack Weatherly, a complicated 75 year old man, you should know that he was formerly homeless, but held substantial inherited wealth as a descendant of Ulysses W. Weatherly, the inventor of the public restroom soap dispenser. Instead, his problems were tied to his mental health – he was too unstable to rent or purchase a home.

Jack also possessed the avocation of breaking into parked cars. And on the first Wednesday morning of September 2008, he walked through the Mission, drifting southeast, until discovering two silver prizes:

A half finished cup of Diet Coke and a scratched Grateful Dead CD

And, after drinking what was left of the beverage, he allowed himself a moment of self-reflection. "This is why I do everything," he said in a whisper.

But his morning wasn't over. With additional luck on the way back, he captured the gold prize:

A yellow tennis ball worn thin by the mouth of a dog

And to celebrate, Jack sprang for a bottle of Dom Pérignon wrapped in a brown paper bag. And after counting his change, he declared to the clerk: "I'm riding the Google Bus today!"

The Google Bus, which shuttles Google employees from neighborhoods that used to be interesting to workplaces suited for children, is not intended for the public at large. But Jack refused to acknowledge boundaries. Instead, he snuck aboard with a promotional sandwich card, picked a satisfactory seat for getting trashed, and subjected everyone not only to *Shakedown Street*, but to *Shakedown Street* skipping repeatedly on a portable stereo that he had thieved in July.

But one passenger eventually complained, prompting the driver to make an announcement:

"To our guest in the back: please refrain from drinking alcoholic beverages and playing loud music aboard the Google Bus. Many of your fellow passengers have important work to attend to while aboard, and continued disturbances will result in your removal."

But Jack did not take the admonition well.

"I'm also working!" Jack shouted back. "I'm putting Eric Schmidt – and now you – onto a Google Doc with a thousand masturbating emoticons. Because this bus belongs to me! And you'll never get a search warrant or a building permit to remove me from my own Google Bus, man!"

Yet the driver did anyway, on the shoulder of Highway 101.

But not all was lost. After regaining his bearings, Jack was pleased to discover himself well-positioned to patronize every dive bar along El Camino Real in central San Mateo County.

And at first, the pursuit held promise. However, Jack soon found himself bored senseless by every bar – all of them with TVs dwelling on the 49ers seven point loss to the San Diego Chargers three days prior. That was, at least, until he discovered a change of scenery at Steamie's Bar in San Mateo. In the very back of Steamie's, near the emergency exit and away from the restrooms, the 2008 Republican National Convention was on instead. And although nobody else was watching, Jack bought a beer and took a seat.

And twenty minutes later, he had the privilege of witnessing a future vice president make his first nationwide address:

"I'm Representative Mike Pence of Indiana and I use he/him pronouns," the man said. "And I'm here today because I won't rest until we have a genderfucked America!"

And of course, the declaration was met with the roaring approval of every delegate in the arena.

Meanwhile, for his part, Jack smiled, bought another beer, and returned two minutes early for a montage honoring former New York City mayor Rudolph Giuliani (now affectionately known to the public as *America's Fuckface*). The video highlighted Giuliani's acts of heroism on the fateful day of September 11, 2001: appearing before microphones and cameras. And at the end of it, there wasn't a dry eye in the house.

It also had an effect on Jack. Though Jack was hardly a Republican (he had voted for Ralph Nader three times in 2000 and five times in 2004), the video delivered him to the San Francisco International Airport by way of Peninsula Returnable Hardware of San Bruno. And at a counter in Terminal 1, he bought a one-way ticket to Oakland by way of Tokyo Narita with no questions asked. But he encountered greater scrutiny at security, where he was stopped by five TSA agents for putting a box cutter and its receipt into his plastic tray. "I'm not a terrorist," Jack tried to explain to them. "I'm just the right person to fly the plane today."

But it was 2008, still too soon to be joking around, and Jack was detained, evaluated, and brought to Herrick.

But that was then. And this is now. Today, Jack finds real estate, and he's good at it. And with one single radio commercial, he even launched a successful small business by leveraging his problems from the past. And the excellent spot, with 30 seconds running time, was put together by his dedicated employees:

"Living with bitterness and anger, without warm showers and no refuge from the weather. Having no patience, and longing for some semblance of dignity. Left for dead on the sidewalk, and desperate for walls, a roof, and some allowance of privacy.

Jack Weatherly can empathize with the frustrations of homebuyers. You want a nice place to live that you can call your own!

That's why Jack Weatherly is here for you. With years in shelters, streets, and alleyways, he's truly an expert

when it comes to looking for a home. As we like to say:
his last box could have been on your next block!"

So, when Jack made time to have drinks with me at his
favorite bar (the legendary Vesuvio Cafe in North
Beach – an establishment separated from City Lights
Bookstore by an alley named in honor of the author
John Grisham), I felt fortunate. And unsurprisingly, he
showed up with twenty books in a City Lights bag, and
was eager to talk about the dissipation of bohemian San
Francisco.

"This city doesn't export poetry anymore," Jack told me
before saying hello. "Shit is happening in Melbourne
and Overland Park, and what are kids doing here?" he
asked. "Finding more dumb shit we can do with our
phones.

"And for everybody listening, here's my insight," he
added after sitting down. "Every techbro here is looking
for a condominium with four rooms: one for wiffleball,
one for violent video games, one for consuming
Grubhub orders, and one for jerking off.

"But guess what else is happening? In western
Massachusetts there's a 28 year old poet who's

amalgamating 19th Century Transcendentalism with the contemporary avant garde. I find his work to be fascinating. He just published a new collection of poems, called *Fuck You.*"

Jack read me the third poem, titled *Montpelier.*

Autumn in New England

leaves

fall

into the pond

In Montpelier,

I paid a prostitute 50 dollars to piss on my face

I was impressed, Jack was pleased with my approval, and we accomplished ten rounds with ambitions for more. But the bouncer was obliged to address the patrons shortly before 2am. "We care where you go," he expressed out of sincere concern for our comfort and welfare. "But we regret that you can't stay here."

But Jack wouldn't call it a night. "There's always a party at the Greyhound station," he said. "We can get there from Stockton and Washington now."

Grisham Alley led to Grant, and then Washington, and then Stockton, but we encountered a construction site once we got there. But, undeterred, Jack had a vision. "We need to jump over these wires, and climb over these fences, just to get out of our comfort zones," he said. And after being cajoled while under the influence, I agreed to go along.

But it didn't take long for us to regret the decision. In our efforts to grow as people, I fell from the second level of scaffolding and Jack from its third. *I shouldn't have listened to Jack and we shouldn't have had those tenths,* I thought.

But we received help expeditiously – and it was help from a very distinguished individual: the world's oldest evicted person. And, understanding the severity of our conditions, he offered us unread copies of the *San Francisco Examiner* to stop our bleeding.

"This will be Chinatown station," he told us, giving both of us clarity. "Someone truly important will explain everything to us soon."

And, sure enough, moments later, he proved to be correct beyond all measure. We were visited not by a customer service representative of the SFMTA, nor by a legislative aide of a member of the Board of Supervisors, but rather by a celestial being – namely, an angel sent from the kingdom of heaven. And after she enchanted all of us simply by showing up, she spoke:

"God is disappointed by how overbudget and overdue this station is," she said. "Divine intervention will be required, and there's a lot of red tape involved with that right now."

And Jack and I were rendered speechless. But having expected her visitation, the oldest man was prepared with questions.

"When it's done, will the blessings of God keep the escalators clean?" he asked.

"There is no hope for that," the angel sighed. "And really, there is no hope for anything on this planet. This assignment has been profoundly disappointing, and I don't want to be here anymore," she sighed again.

But, however insulting the angel's comments regarding us were, none of us had time to take offense. Because, within seconds, she was overshadowed by a more intriguing figure: a bearded 22-year old white man with a tote bag and a clipboard. And he jogged directly towards us with all of his might, longing to talk.

"What's up guys? Do you have two minutes for humanity?" he asked us casually. "Because I work for HumanityPeople. We collect donations from people and give them to humanity."

And almost reflexively, Jack and I laughed, having heard similar pitches many times before. But the oldest man was clearly moved and offered everything in his pockets: one dollar and nineteen cents in change. "Every young man should have a dream," he said.

So, guilt-ridden, Jack and I reversed course and pitched in.

I provided my credit card number to the young man (4144-7766-2423-3924), expiration date (11/24), and CVV (525). But Jack was unable to retrieve any of his methods of payment after his fall. So, sheepishly, he asked the angel to lend him a twenty dollar bill. And, although she handed the money over, it was not without a protest. "This is bullshit," she said. "And I need to go."

But the angel's abrupt departure gave the young man a new mission: recruiting us to canvass for his secular cause. And, although Jack and I refused to provide anything beyond our financial support, he enlisted the oldest man quite easily. And together, they searched for donations until dawn, leaving Jack and I alone together – at the very moment of autumn's first rain. And after enough drops reached the ground, Jack had something poignant to say about the event:

"It's here. It's the first rain of the season. Six months of shit on the sidewalk – shit of birds, shit of people, shit of rats, and shit of dogs – is finally getting washed into the bay," he said.

"It's beautiful," I replied.

"It's redemption," Jack replied. And then he began to cry.

I gave Jack a huge hug, but to provide more meaningful help, I racked my mind to determine the underlying cause of his sadness. But then I remembered something: In the 1970s, Jack's father was a volunteer meteorologist for the Center for Investigative

Reporting, but was killed while trying to report true weather in Central America. And for Jack, the arrival of low pressure systems often brought back sentimental recollections of his upbringing. And in the process of regaining his composure, Jack recalled to me his most meaningful one:

"40 years before my father passed away, he gave me some advice," Jack said. "*Jack*, he told me: *to win a pissing contest you've got to focus on the size of your bladder, not the size of your penis.*"

"And that's true," I said in appreciation of the story.

"Yes, and it's still true today," Jack replied.

But, despite understanding my responsibility to care for Jack, at one point I allowed my mind to wander for several minutes. And during my neglect, I had failed to notice something critical: Jack was beyond grief. Instead, he was in despair. And it was all made clear with one question:

"Do you know what you want to do with your afterlife?" Jack asked.

And my answer was in the affirmative. "I do," I told him. "I want to run a nightclub on a moon in whatever galaxy I'm allowed to occupy, saving one seat for David Berman and another for Muhammad Ali," I explained.

But needless to say, although I was content with the hereafter, Jack was struggling to find a point to eternal life. So, with love in my heart and concern on my mind, I posed to him the same question. But Jack could only shake his head. And I will never be able to shake his answer:

"I just don't know anymore," he said.